Pick a Pet

Written by Diane Namm

Illustrated by Maribel Suárez

My First
READER

children's press ®

A Division of Scholastic Inc.
New York Toronto London Auckland Sydney
Mexico City New Delhi Hong Kong
Danbury, Connecticut

Library of Congress Cataloging-in-Publication Data

Namm, Diane.
  Pick a pet / written by Diane Namm ; illustrated by Maribel Suárez.
      p. cm. – (My first reader)
Summary: Choosing a pet as her birthday gift proves to be difficult for a young girl as she and her
parents visit a zoo, a farm-animal petting zoo, and a pet store searching for the very best animal friend.
  ISBN 0-516-24417-5 (lib. bdg.)   0-516-25507-X (pbk.)
  [1. Pets–Fiction. 2. Animals–Fiction. 3. Birthdays–Fiction. 4. Hispanic Americans–Fiction.
5. Stories in rhyme.] I. Suárez, Maribel, 1952- ill. II. Title. III. Series.
  PZ8.3.N27Pi 2004
  [E]–dc22
                                   2003014069

1 2 3 4 5 6 7 8 9 10 R 13 12 11 10 09 08 07 06 05 04

Note to Parents and Teachers

Once a reader can recognize and identify the 44 words used to tell this story, he or she will be able to successfully read the entire book. These 44 words are repeated throughout the story, so that young readers will be able to recognize the words easily and understand their meaning.

The 44 words used in this book are:

a	get	me	rat
be	have	monkey	really
bear	I	of	right
can	is	one	see
cat	just	out	should
chick	kitten	panda	some
could	let's	pet	that
fish	like	pick	the
for	lion	picking	there
free	lots	pig	which
fun	maybe	pony	would

LIONS

PANDAS

I can pick a pet. Just one.

A monkey could be lots of fun.

I could pick a panda bear.

Could I have that lion there?

Picking out a pet is fun!

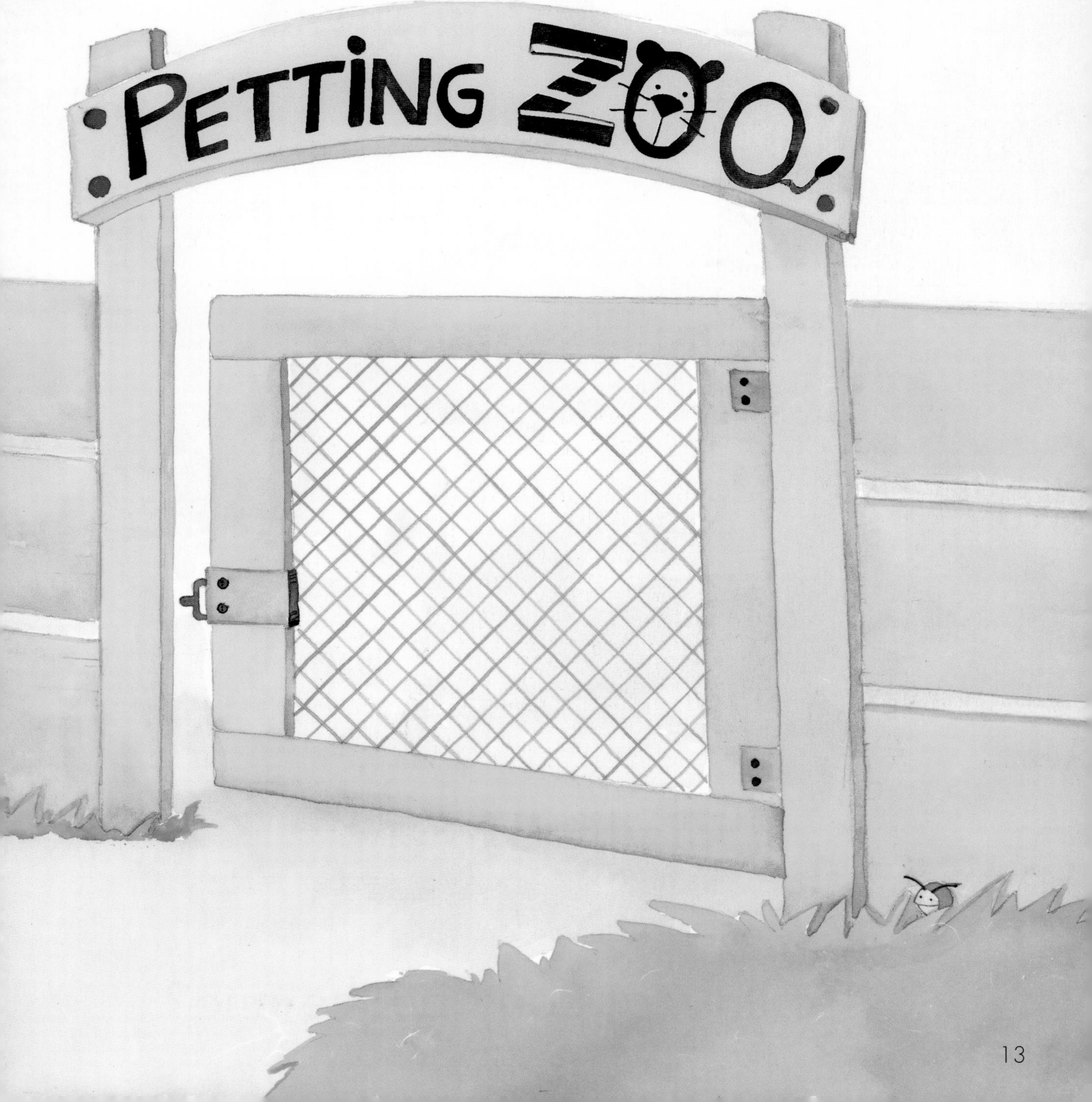
PETTING ZOO

Could that pony be the one?

15

A pig could be the pet I pick.

Maybe I should get a chick.

Which pet is the one for me?

PETS

I could get some fish for free.

Maybe I should get a rat.

I would really like a cat!

Which cat should I pick?

Let's see.

A kitten is just right for me!

ABOUT THE AUTHOR

Diane Namm is the author of over twenty-five books for children and young adults. Formerly an editor in New York, Namm freelances for a children's entertainment production company, writes, and lives in Malibu, California, with her husband and two children. When Namm's children were little, they looked in every pet store and animal shelter in Los Angeles to find a perfect pet for them— just like the little girl in this book.

ABOUT THE ILLUSTRATOR

Maribel Suárez has enjoyed drawing ever since she was little. She s   ed Industrial Design at UNAM in Mexico and received a Master's Degree in Design Research from the Royal College in London, England. Suárez has been illustrating children's books since 1985. She's had more than sixty books published in Mexico, the United States, and Spain. She lives in Mexico City with her three children and one of her greatest pleasures is to travel with them all around the world.